Animal Sleepyheads:
1 to 10

Animal Sleepyheads:
1 to 10

By Joanna Cole
Pictures by Jeni Bassett

SCHOLASTIC
HARDCOVER
SCHOLASTIC INC./New York

Library of Congress Cataloging-in-Publication Data
Cole, Joanna.
Animal sleepyheads.
Summary: Sleepy animals introduce the numbers from
one to ten.
[1. Animals—Fiction. 2. Sleep—Fiction. 3. Stories
in rhyme. 4. Counting] I. Bassett, Jeni, ill.
II. Title.
PZ8.3.C673An   1988   [E]   87-9813
ISBN 0-590-40919-0

12   11   10   9   8   7   6   5   4   3   2   8   9/8   0   1   2   3/9

Printed in the U.S.A.   36

First Scholastic printing, February 1988

1 sleepy bunny
curled up
soft and snug,

2

sleepy puppy dogs
dreaming on a rug,

3

sleepy polar bears
snoozing in the snow,

4

sleepy pussycats
purring high and low,

sleepy elephants
tucked in big bunk beds.

Whisper softly,
everyone—
don't wake
those sleepyheads!

6

sleepy kangaroos
carried by their mamas,

sleepy tigers
wearing striped pajamas,

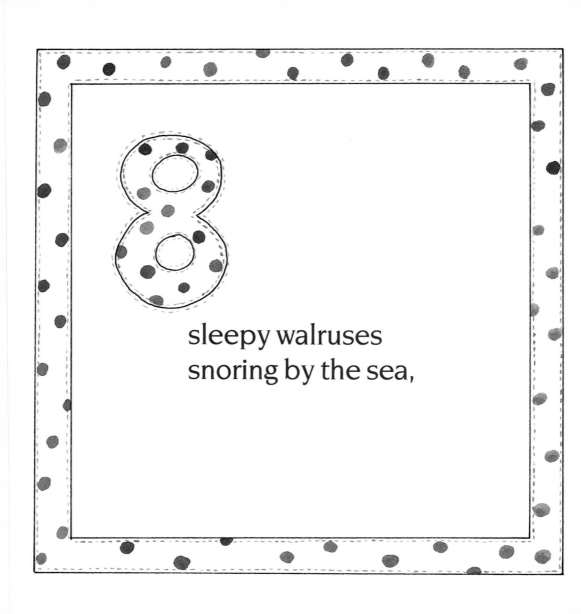

8

sleepy walruses
snoring by the sea,

sleepy possums
hanging in a tree,

10

sleepy mice
squeezed in just one bed.

Count them all,
now close your eyes.

Sweet dreams,
my sleepyhead!